MIKE'S TOADS

BUFO
AMERICANUS

Weekly Reader Children's Book Club Presents

MIKE'S TOADS

by WILSON GAGE

Illustrated by GLEN ROUNDS

THE WORLD PUBLISHING COMPANY

NEW YORK AND CLEVELAND

Published by The World Publishing Company
110 East 59th Street, New York, New York 10022
Published simultaneously in Canada by
Nelson, Foster & Scott Ltd.
Library of Congress catalog card number: 77-101845
Text copyright © 1970 by Wilson Gage
Illustrations copyright © 1970 by Glen Rounds
Designed by Jack Jaget
Weekly Reader Children's Book Club Edition
Intermediate Division

To Arthur,

with dearest love always

MIKE'S TOADS

WHEN MIKE walked into the fifth-grade room Ruthie Osmundson was talking to Mrs. Woodall. Mrs. Woodall looked worried, in fact she looked distracted. Mike thought distracted was a good word. His mother was always being distracted. And Mike had figured out that being distracted was doing what Mrs. Woodall was trying to do now: make your mind go two ways at once. Mrs. Woodall was trying to listen to Ruthie and trying to think of something else at the same time. Mike wondered what on earth Ruthie could be saying to Mrs. Woodall.

9

He went over to his desk and was going to sit down when Steve hollered, "Hey, Mike," and held something up for him to see. Mike went over to Steve's desk and looked.

"What is it?" he asked.

"It's a spearhead," said Steve. "An Indian spearhead. My uncle sent it to me. He went back in a cave near where he lives. He went back inside about a thousand miles, I guess, and he found all these good Indian things and bones and stuff. And he sent me this. It must be about a thousand years old, my uncle says."

Mike gazed down at the narrow piece of flint on Steve's hand, with its edges roughly chipped in small scallops. How old *was* a thousand years, anyhow? How long ago? There must have been dinosaurs around maybe.

George Anderson leaned over Steve's shoulder and looked too. "I bet it's not much good," he said. "It's broken."

Steve laughed loudly. "Dumbhead, it wouldn't be a spearhead if it wasn't chipped," he cried.

George drew his heavy eyebrows down and turned purple the way he always did when he got mad. "You're the dumbhead," he retorted. "I wasn't talking about the chipped-out places. I was talking about that!" He pointed to the corner of the upper end, where a small piece really was broken off.

Steve opened his mouth to say something else and then the bell rang and Mrs. Woodall said, "George, would you open that last window?" and everybody else scrambled to get to his desk or put his books away or take them out

or do whatever it was he wanted to do before Mrs. Woodall called the roll.

And as soon as she had called it she started looking distracted again.

"Now listen," she said as she put the roll book down
on her desk. "Ruthie's mother can't take her car out to
the planetarium tomorrow afternoon. She planned to take
five people. Can any of you whose mothers offered to drive
squeeze another passenger or two into your cars?"

Everybody looked at Mrs. Woodall and finally Gary Sutton said he guessed he could.

"Oh, Gary," said Mrs. Woodall. "You're already taking seven people and that's really too many."

"Maybe some of them will be sick tomorrow," Gary said hopefully.

Mrs. Woodall frowned. "I don't think we ought to count on that," she answered.

And then Mike held up his hand. "I'll take them," he said. "Or anyway my mother will. We've got a nine-passenger station wagon."

Mrs. Woodall smiled. "That would be grand," she said. "That would mean Gary's mother would only have to have six people in her car. But I think you'd better ask your mother first, Mike. It might not be convenient."

"Oh, she'll be glad to, Mrs. Woodall," Mike answered. "She said so." And she had said so. Mike had been absent the day Mrs. Woodall asked for cars to take the class to the planetarium. And when he had found out about it and told his mother he was going with Gary Sutton, she had said it was too bad Mike hadn't been there that day because she would have been glad to drive.

"Well, it would certainly be a help," said Mrs. Woodall. "So many mothers are taking the little ones to the Reading Center tomorrow afternoon, and there's the junior high baseball game, and that makes it hard to find cars. I do appreciate that, Mike."

"Sure," said Mike. He felt very good and generous and it didn't matter that five minutes later he had to say he couldn't do this new kind of arithmetic problem Mrs. Woodall had been talking about yesterday.

When Mike got home, his cat, Ribby, was lying asleep in the sun on the sidewalk. He walked over to her and she woke up and rolled over on her back and showed her fat white stomach. Daddy said Ribby was the most mis-named cat in the world. She didn't even *have* any ribs. Sometimes Mike worried about her. Last week he had measured her and she was twenty-one inches long and eighteen inches around.

Now he picked her up, and she certainly was heavy. Maybe she ought to go on a diet or something. But he bet she wouldn't eat tomatoes and lettuce, the way his mother did when she went on a diet.

In the house his mother was sitting at the dining-room table but she wasn't eating tomatoes and lettuce—or any-thing else. She was cutting leaves and birds and flowers out of gold paper. The Public Library was having a fiftieth anniversary tea and Mother was one of the ladies who were helping make the decorations.

"Mother," said Mike. "Do you think Ribby ought to go on a diet?"

"Goodness," said Mother, holding up something she had just cut out, "do you think there really are butterflies shaped like this? It looks more like some kind of insulator to me."

"But do you think so?" persisted Mike. "She's awful heavy."

"She ought to do more work instead of lying around

sleeping all day," said Mother severely. "She ought to help me with these decorations—and so should you, Mike. I'm never going to have them finished in time. Mrs. Hamilton wants me to bring them over tomorrow afternoon and start making them into ropes and garlands, and I've only done the birds and about half the flowers. And these awful butterflies—"

Mike had a sudden sinking feeling somewhere under his third shirt button. "Tomorrow afternoon!" he cried, dropping Ribby to the floor. "*All* afternoon?"

Mother turned and looked at him very steadily. Finally she said, "Mike, what have you done now?"

"Well, gosh, you said you'd be glad to," said Mike. "And I just told Mrs. Woodall what you said."

"Be glad to do what?" exclaimed Mother. "Do try to make sense."

"You said you'd be glad to take some of the class out to the planetarium tomorrow afternoon," Mike said carefully. "And Ruthie's mother can't do it tomorrow, her car's in the shop. And Mrs. Woodall said who could do it and nobody could do it, and we've got a station wagon, and you said you'd be glad to and . . ."

"Oh, Mike," said Mother reproachfully. "When are you ever going to learn? How many times have you gotten into trouble saying somebody else would be glad to do things, without finding out whether they could or whether they want to or . . ."

Mike put his books down on one of the dining-room chairs and sat down at the table.

"I'll help," he offered. "I'll cut out butterflies all afternoon

14

and all night and everything. Gosh, somebody had to help Mrs. Woodall out. There wasn't anybody else who could do it."

Mother sighed. "I'd love to have you help," she answered. "Flowers are what I need—here's the pattern. But helping out won't change the fact that I do have to go to Mrs. Hamilton's tomorrow afternoon. Fortunately Daddy will be home early so he can take you to the planetarium. It won't be what he planned to do with his afternoon off, but I guess he'll be willing to help out Mrs. Woodall. Still, you remember last time you did something like this."

Mike did remember. Daddy had really hit the ceiling. But at the time it had seemed like a good thing to do. When Mrs. Henderson had come over from across the street and asked if she could pick some flowers to take to her sister in the hospital, Mike had said sure, his daddy had plenty of roses, he wouldn't mind if Mrs. Henderson picked some.

The trouble was Mrs. Henderson picked all the buds Daddy had been planning to enter in the rose show that very afternoon. When he saw the bushes he just yelled. It scared Mike out of his wits to hear his daddy just open his mouth and yell like that. It didn't do any good for Mike to explain over and over that he felt sorry for Mrs. Henderson's sister in the hospital, shut up in that smelly place when the outside world was full of spring and grass and roses. And it didn't do any good to explain that he hadn't known Mrs. Henderson was going to pick those particular roses.

Daddy just went on yelling and yelling. He didn't do

anything to Mike, like say he couldn't watch TV, or make him rake leaves all afternoon, or even smack him. But for a week he could hardly look at Mike, and when he did he frowned, and Mike thought it was the worst thing that had ever happened to him. So you'd think he'd remember, wouldn't you?

"If you could just remember," Mother said now, "not to volunteer other people's services. All you have to do is wait till you can ask me or Daddy if it's all right to do something. I don't mind a bit taking people out to the planetarium, I *would* have been glad to, if I had known. But I've already agreed to do this with Mrs. Hamilton and we've made all sorts of arrangements, and it's too late to change now.... Well, I guess Daddy will just have to do it. Mrs. Woodall needs the help, I know."

Mike didn't answer. He picked up the scissors and started cutting out funny-looking flowers and he cut them out and cut them out, all afternoon, even though it was a perfectly nice day outside and even though Mrs. Woodall had given him some extra problems to work in arithmetic.

At the supper table he could hardly eat because he knew he was going to have to tell Daddy about tomorrow afternoon. He just sat there beside his brother David, looking at his chicken, till Daddy said, "David, did you try those new hedge clippers last weekend? I think I'll use them tomorrow afternoon if they're easier to handle than the old ones."

And then Mother said, "Oh, no, you won't," and looked at Mike. He had to tell then about Mrs. Woodall needing somebody to drive five people and Mother saying she'd be glad to and the station wagon and everything.

Daddy glared at Mike and at Mother and at the ceiling and then he said, "Where do I have to drive?" and Mike said, "To the planetarium. It's next door to the Children's Museum."

"The planetarium?" cried David. "Neat-o. It's great, Daddy, it really is. They've got a telescope that's got a twenty-four-inch reflector. And neat pictures of the moon and Venus and places."

David was fourteen and almost in high school. Stars and rocks and gravity and all that stuff were what he was interested in. He never had any trouble with arithmetic. Mostly he and Mike didn't get along too well, but now Mike was certainly glad he had a brother like David. Daddy started asking questions and ended up looking rather pleased with a chance to see the planetarium.

Still Mike wasn't taking any chances. All day he kept warning the people that they had to be out on the sidewalk as soon as school was over, so Daddy wouldn't have to wait. And when the bell rang Mike went and stood right beside George, because George was so slow and always the last person to leave and having to go back for his sweater or his workbook or something.

David had been right. The planetarium was great. When Mike first heard about the planetarium he had imagined it was like an aquarium full of little suns and moons and planets. He still thought this would be a pretty good idea. In his mind's eye he could see all those little comets and stars whizzing around inside their glass home, and he wished he had one.

But the real thing was great too. He was so interested he hardly poked Steve, sitting in front of him in the dark, more than once every five minutes. It was all about the Equinox and the Milky Way and falling stars, and Mike felt very intelligent and educated when he came blinking out into the daylight. Daddy had liked it too and he talked to everybody in the car about it and didn't seem to mind that he had to wait while George went back inside and looked for his sweater. It wasn't till he got home and looked at the hedge, grown up every which way, that he got a little cross.

Mike was relieved. It had worked out better than he could have hoped. And in two weeks school was out and Mike was in the sixth grade, where he never thought he'd get to be, and vacation was just beginning. Life was so pleasant he just forgot to be careful. At least afterward he figured that must have been what happened. Because that Wednesday afternoon, when David was at the movies and Mother was in town and his sister Claire was sitting up in a tree in the backyard reading a book, Mike was the only one who even saw Bobby Madison coming up to the front door.

Mike was standing in the hall at the foot of the steps and he saw Bobby out on the sidewalk, and he went and looked through the screen door, and Bobby looked back. "Hi," said Bobby. "Hi," said Mike. He'd only seen Bobby once or twice in his life. Bobby was David's age but they didn't seem to be particular friends or anything.

Still, Bobby must be looking for David. "Dave's gone to the movies," Mike said.

"Oh," said Bobby. "Well. What'd he go to see?"

"I don't know," Mike answered. "I was gone when he left."

"Oh," said Bobby. "Well. I wanted to see him. I was wondering if he'd do something for me." He stopped and Mike said, "I guess he would," and Bobby said, "I'm going to California tomorrow. I mean the day after tomorrow. And I wanted somebody to look after my terrariums while I was gone. I was wondering if David would do it. It's not any trouble, just feeding the toads once in a while."

"Well, sure, I guess so," said Mike.

Bobby looked relieved. "Gosh, thanks," he said. "I'll bring 'em over tomorrow about lunchtime."

"O.K.," said Mike.

That night Mike was climbing into bed when he remembered. He got out of bed and went next door to David's room. David was sitting at his desk reading a book and squeezing his rubber ball to make his muscles bigger.

"I forgot," said Mike. "Bobby Madison came over here this afternoon and asked if you would take care of his terrariums because he's going to California."

"What'd you tell him?" asked David.

"I told him I guessed you would," answered Mike.

David dropped his ball.

"Oh, you did!" he cried. "Well, Mr. Dumbhead, here's something else you forgot. I'm going to camp, remember? I'm going to be gone about five weeks, remember? And I didn't say anything to Bobby Madison. So I guess you're the one who's going to have to look after the terrariums!"

LYING IN THE DARK, Mike thought about what David had said. He'd never have to do it. He didn't know one thing about taking care of terrariums. And he was just a little kid, even if he was in the sixth grade. A high-school boy like Bobby Madison wouldn't want a little kid taking care of his terrariums. Especially a little kid who didn't even know how.

In the morning he would call Bobby and tell him about Dave going off to camp, and Bobby would say, "Oh. Well. I guess I'll have to get somebody else to look after them. Goodbye." And that would be that.

At least Mike hoped that would be that. He had troubles enough this summer without taking care of any old terrariums. There was his bicycle, for instance. His good bicycle with five speeds and high-rise handlebars that he hadn't been able to ride since March because of leaving it on the school playground where the milk truck could run over it.

He had just left it there a minute and felt sure he'd be back in time to move it before the milkman came out of the cafeteria and drove off. Only somehow he hadn't. And even though the milk truck only drove over it a little bit, such a little bit that the milkman hadn't even noticed, getting it fixed cost more than Mike had ever dreamed it would.

Daddy said he couldn't afford to have it fixed, not after what he had paid for that bicycle to begin with. Mother said that they ought to be able to work something out, and what they worked out was that Mike would pay for the repairs by working for Daddy at sixty cents an hour. When he had worked out half the price of repairs, Daddy would have the bike fixed so he could have it to ride while he was still working out the other half.

The only trouble was that Daddy was so fussy about what he would let Mike do, and Mike had so little time during school, that so far he had only made two dollars and thirty-seven cents.

And arithmetic was another worrisome thing. Mrs. Woodall kept saying that Mike was one of those people who needed more practice in arithmetic than she had time to give them. Mother tried to get somebody to help him this summer but she couldn't find anybody, so she was doing it herself. Three hours a week she sat down and went over all those problems with Mike and tried to help. Mike appreciated it, but he didn't think it was doing a bit of good. Still, he spent a lot of time at it, finding his book and his workbook and pencils and paper and stuff. All these things just about filled up his week, so he just wouldn't be able to take care of the terrariums.

With this thought he turned over and went to sleep. And

the next day terrariums were the very last thing on his mind, all that bright warm morning. He had plenty of other things to think about, as always, including arithmetic. He'd just had his deviled ham sandwich and apple salad, a very dull lunch, and Mother had just sat down beside him and started talking about these division problems, when Bobby Madison's mother drove up in front of the house and Bobby Madison got out of the car. Mother looked out the window. "Isn't that Bobby Madison?" she asked. "What does he want?"

"Oh, good grief!" said Mike. "I forgot."

It was too late to call now. Bobby had already got one of the terrariums out of the trunk of the car and was lugging it up the front walk. Mike scowled. Rats! Why couldn't he have remembered to call?

"What in the world?" said Mother and Mike got up and ran to the front door. Bobby stood there with the terrarium in his arms. So that was what a terrarium looked like. It was an aquarium. After the planetarium had turned out to be what it was, Mike hadn't even tried to imagine what a terrarium was. And now it turned out to be just an aquarium with some mud and gravel and wilted ferns in the bottom.

"Gee, Bobby, I'm sorry," Mike cried. "I meant to call you. David's going to camp. He can't take care of your terrariums. I was going to tell you first thing this morning and I forgot."

Bobby looked horrified. "But you said he'd do it," he almost yelled. "And I'm leaving tomorrow—tomorrow morning, early. And I can't find anybody else to do it!"

"Do what?" asked Mother. Bobby just stood there clutching the terrarium, and Mike had to explain. He could see Mother was pretty mad. "Well, you've done it again," she said when he had finished. She opened the screen door and said, "Come on in, Bobby. It's true that David's going to be gone. But since Mike told you the terrariums would be looked after, he can do it himself. He's perfectly capable and I'll see that he does a good job." Mike started to say that he could do a good job without her supervision, but then he decided not to. She sounded really terribly mad.

Bobby grinned and came squeezing in the door. "Anyway, I'd have sense enough to turn sideways if I was carrying an aquarium through a door," Mike told himself.

"It's not much trouble taking care of them," Bobby explained. "They're really easy to take care of. My mother wouldn't have let me ask somebody else to do it if it had been any trouble. She'd have made me let them go."

"Well. I'm sure Mike can manage very well," Mother said, and she let the screen door close and went off toward the kitchen.

Mike looked at Bobby, and Bobby said, "Where'll I put this?" And Mike said, "I guess it had better go in my room."

Mike liked his room. It was pretty big, even though on one side the roof slanted down till it was only about four feet off the floor. That part of the room was plenty good for bookcases and boxes of stuff. He and Bobby put the terrarium on top of the bookcases, right next to the windows so the toads would get some sun. "But they mustn't have too much sun," Bobby pointed out. "If they get too hot, they dry up and die. That's why they have to have plants and stones to get under, so they can keep cool and moist."

"Gee," said Mike. He couldn't think of anything else to say.

Bobby got the terrarium settled the way he thought it should be and then he went down and brought up another one. The second one had four tiny little creatures in it. It was planted with moss and ferns and some other things. None of the plants looked very lively. The animals, on the other hand, leaped around like popcorn. Bobby said there were four of them, but Mike didn't see how he could be sure.

"I hatched these from tadpoles," Bobby said proudly.

"Hatched?" repeated Mike in surprise.

"Well, you know," said Bobby. "I found the tadpoles and took care of them and they grew up to be these things." He leaned over and squinted in at them. "It's hard to get a good look at them. They only quit being tadpoles about five days ago. I wish they'd hold still a minute so I could get a good look at them. I may make these my science fair project for next year and I'd like to get a good look at them."

Just about that time Bobby's mother blew her horn for the third time. Bobby went on hurriedly. "The way I feed them is, I take off this cover and then I put a piece of sort of rotten banana or something in the cage with them, and then I put this screen over the top. Lots of those little flies that come around rotten bananas go in and the little toads eat them, or at least they're supposed to. I've never seen

26

it happen. But you got to remember not to leave the
banana in there too long because it might get really rotten
and that might not be good for them."

There were three toads in the other terrarium, like the
three bears, a little one and a middle-sized one and a big
one. The big one looked as big around as a plate and was
as ugly and warty and fierce-looking as a rhinoceros.

"Will it bite?" Mike asked and Bobby looked surprised.

"They don't have any teeth, stupid," he answered kindly.

"Oh," said Mike. "Well, then how do they eat?"

"You can catch flies and things and put them in there with them," Bobby went on, not quite understanding what Mike meant. "But that's hard. The easiest thing is to put some cheese or a little dog food or fish or hamburger or something on the end of a broom straw and wiggle it around until they reach out and grab it and swallow it. It's neat to see them eat."

Bobby's mother honked again. "Gosh, I got to go, she'll kill me. Be sure they have water. You put it in those dishes I've got in there. Mr. MacMillan can help you, you know, the science teacher at junior high. Goodbye, I'll be back in August."

"Goodbye," said Mike. He didn't go to the door with Bobby, but he heard him clattering downstairs and the door of his car slam. Mike stood there staring in at the big toad. The toad stared back. Once in a while it swallowed a little and blinked its gold eyes. Mike sighed. He didn't think he was going to care much for these toads.

Mother came in and stood beside him. She had mostly forgotten about being angry, he could tell. After a minute she said, "Goodness, that's the most hideous creature I ever saw except the Steeles' bulldog."

"I guess it can't help it," said Mike. "It's eyes are pretty though."

Mother bent down to look. She was already bending down pretty far anyway because of the sloping roof. She and Mike peered in at the toad, which obligingly turned sideways so they could see its eyes, liquid gold, gleaming, with the black oval-shaped pupil floating in it, deep and mysterious and winking.

" 'The toad, ugly and venomous, wears yet a precious jewel in his head,' " Mother said, and Mike said, "What?"

Mother laughed. "Something I learned in school," she said. "It's true, isn't it? I don't think that eye is what the poet meant, but it truly is beautiful. Still, the rest of the beast is pretty awful."

"I guess toads really do give you warts," said Mike. "Look how many it's got. It's given itself about a million."

"Oh, I think that's just superstition," said Mother. "I'll ask Dr. Miller when I take you all in for boosters."

At the thought of those needles Mike's stomach knotted up, but he knew it wasn't possible to get out of it. And it probably didn't hurt as much as thinking about it did. At least he hoped it didn't.

He turned away from the terrariums, and Mother took him by the shoulder. "Now, Mike," she said. "There's one thing I want you to remember. These animals are absolutely dependent on you. They cannot get out of those tanks and get their own water and food. They can't yell or scream or do anything like that. *You* are the one who has to take care of them. It isn't their fault that you told Bobby that David would do it and David couldn't. I hope you are going to be kindhearted enough to take care of them without me reminding you, even if you shouldn't be grown-up enough."

Mike thought that was a mean thing for Mother to say.

He was plenty grown-up enough, he always remembered to feed Ribby and bring her in on cold nights. Or almost always.

"Now come along, let's finish up that arithmetic," Mother said.

That afternoon David came into Mike's room to see the terrariums. "Neat," he said. He looked at them awhile, then he said, "I guess you know that toads are amphibians."

"Sure," said Mike, though he hadn't known it. He didn't really know it now, because he hadn't the slightest idea what amphibians were, but he wasn't going to let David tell him. Just then Claire came in and looked at the terrariums but she didn't say anything. Claire hardly ever said anything.

When Daddy came home he went upstairs to see them too. He frowned. "Those things are planted all wrong," he said.

"This one's got the little bitty toads in it," Mike pointed out.

"That's bracken and it needs more sun. It's drowning in all that water," Daddy went on.

"Look at this big one, Daddy," said Mike.

"What you need in there is some philodendron and some spleenwort and a piece of rotten wood with some polypody ferns."

"They have nice eyes," said Mike, but he didn't have much hope that Daddy was listening to him.

"Tell you what," proposed Daddy. "This weekend I'll clean the cases out and replant them properly. It'll be much better for the toads."

"Gee, Daddy, you noticed!" cried Mike.

"Noticed what?" asked Daddy.

"That there were toads in there," said Mike. And Daddy laughed and pulled his hair and went out, bumping his head on the ceiling.

Mike was going to the ball game that night with Steve and Steve's father. But just before supper it began to rain. At first it was just a little misty rain, a fine sprinkle, but by the time Mike had finished his chocolate pudding it was coming down hard. Mike called Steve on the phone and Steve said gloomily that his father guessed the game was called off. "Why don't you come over here and spend the night?" Steve asked after a long silence.

Mike thought. "You better come over here," he said finally. "I've got all these terrariums to take care of." He stopped. "Wait a minute, I'd better ask my mother if it's all right."

Mother said it was all right, and Steve came over. He and Mike went upstairs and looked at the toads and then they went downstairs and watched a TV program about some children marooned on Venus. It was a stupid program and anyway Mike had already seen it once. He only watched because Steve wanted to.

When the program ended they went to bed because there didn't seem to be anything else to do. Mike had a double bed on account of the sloping ceiling in his room. Bunk beds didn't fit and there wasn't wall space for twin beds.

He and Steve got in bed and Mike pulled up the sheet. At the open window the rain rushed and whispered and dripped and dropped. Mike was suddenly very sleepy.

Steve threw back the sheet and raised his feet in the air till his legs in their blue-patterned pajamas were sticking straight up. Slowly, with many sighs and grunts, he lowered his legs to the mattress. After a minute he raised them again.

"What in the world are you doing?" asked Mike. He was a little bit scared. For a second he thought Steve was having some kind of fit or something.

"I'm doing my exercises," Steve answered, panting. "I do them every night, but I keep forgetting to do them till after I get in bed."

"Oh," said Mike. Then he said, "I spent the night at your house last week and you weren't doing exercises then."

"I only started doing them last night," explained Steve, flinging out an arm and hitting Mike heavily in the chest.

"Oh," said Mike and moved over to the edge of the bed. He lay there listening to Steve puffing and listening to the rain falling and all of a sudden there was another noise in the room, a noise that Mike had never heard before, a weird sad sound, a long-drawn-out chirring trill.

Steve sat up right in the middle of one of his exercises and nearly fell out of bed. "What was that?" he asked in a loud whisper.

Mike was going to say, "Yikes, I don't know," and then he thought of the toads. "The toads," he whispered back. "It must have been one of the toads." He found his flashlight under the bed and turned it on, and he and Steve crept over to the terrarium with the big toads in it. Mike shone the beam in on the drooping ferns. The light came to rest on the middle-sized toad and it blinked and looked sleepy. And then it seemed to take a breath and its leathery

little throat swelled out like a bubble and it made that sweet, strange melancholy sound.

"Gosh," thought Mike. "Mother was wrong. They can yell all right."

"Gee," said Steve.

After a while they got back in bed. Mike was relieved to find that Steve had forgotten about exercises. The rain came down, the toad called twice more, and the boys fell asleep.

Steve had said he would help Mike feed the toads in the morning. But somehow after breakfast they got to fooling around and suddenly it was nearly twelve o'clock and Steve had to go home. Mike went in the kitchen to ask Mother if it was time for lunch and she said, "Mike, did you feed those toads?"

"I was just going to," he answered and went over to the pantry and got the ripest of the bananas out of the fruit bin. He peeled it and looked at it sharply to see if it was a little bit rotten and decided that it was. He carried it upstairs and took the glass top off the smaller terrarium and put the banana down on the moss at the bottom. Then he put the screen top over the glass case and fitted it neatly. He stared in at the tiny toads. At first he couldn't see them at all and then he saw one of them glued to the glass right in front of him. It was hardly bigger than a fly and it clung to the smooth wall with tiny muddy feet. He could see now that they had been all over the glass; little tracks of their damp feet and fat little bellies were left wherever they had landed.

After a minute he turned to the other terrarium. There was the great toad, squatting and blinking. There was the middle-sized toad, looking smug and pleased. "I guess it liked raising all that fuss in the night," Mike thought.

But where was the smallest toad? Mike peered into the terrarium. This one had hardly any plants in it and they were pretty spindly so it was easy to look into. But there wasn't a sign of the little toad.

"Oh, help," said Mike aloud and took off the glass cover and pushed aside the weedy ferns. He picked up the two rocks and dug around among the larger pebbles. The middle-sized toad hopped around but the large one simply sat and occasionally swallowed. It looked horribly fat and full and contented.

"He ate it," thought Mike, horrified. "He got hungry and he swallowed the little one. Oh, yikes, everybody will kill me!"

MAYBE it would be easier if he killed himself. He'd just open the window and jump out and lie there dead on the grass. Only it wouldn't work. He knew, because once George had fallen out of that window. George was too fat to sit on a windowsill. He had rolled up against the screen and the screen had come unfastened and George had just rolled out. Mike remembered the horrifying sight of George's feet and legs disappearing. He'd thought he was going to faint.

And it hadn't even hurt George. He wasn't even bruised. Daddy said it was because George was so well padded and Mother said it was because Daddy's grass was so thick and springy. George said it was because he was tough, and he went around bragging about it for weeks. He made Mike sick.

Anyway, he knew it wasn't any use jumping out the window. And it wasn't any use running away from home; he was old enough to know that was a dumb thing to try. Not that he really wanted to run away, he *liked* home.

But he was going to be in deep trouble when everybody

found out about the little toad. He stared at the biggest toad and it gave him a solemn wink. "Blah," said Mike and stuck his tongue out at it.

Then he had a thought. Maybe he could find another toad and replace the little one before anybody noticed it was gone. He guessed Bobby Madison didn't care whether he had the same toads as long as he had three of them.

He'd have to hurry though. Mother would be after him all day about feeding those toads. She would come up here to make sure he'd done it, sooner or later, and she'd find out.

He sneaked downstairs and went out in the back yard. Claire was up in that tree reading again. He stood under her and caught hold of her foot.

"Lemme borrow your bike," he said.

Claire didn't even look up from her book. She was awful.

"I'll give you half of my bubble gum funnies," he bargained. Claire read on for a second and just as he was opening his mouth to say, "Aw, come on, Claire, I *got* to have a bike," she answered, "All of them."

"All of them!" howled Mike. He'd been collecting for months and had some that nobody else had. However, he didn't have much choice, and it was no use arguing with Claire, she never changed her mind. "O.K., all of them," he said sulkily and ran over to the garage and got out Claire's bike.

It wasn't a good bike like his, it was heavy and awkward and it just had plain old handlebars. At least it wasn't a girl's bike, that was some consolation. It wasn't a girl's bike because it had been bought for David many years ago and handed down to Claire, who didn't much care what she rode.

Mike pedaled as fast as he could. He had a long way to go. He had to go past Steve's house and past George's house and past the school and half a mile beyond the school, where there weren't any sidewalks and the road was full of holes. But at last he was there.

"There" was a big fenced-in field with two cows and a pond in it. The field and the pond and the cows all belonged to Mrs. Thingummy with the geraniums. Mike had been here several times with his father to see the old lady who lived in a small house all crowded with potted geraniums on the other side of this field. Daddy couldn't ever remember her name and always spoke of her as "Mrs. Thingummy with the geraniums." He'd done it so long that Mike couldn't ever think of her as anything else. Still, it was her pond that had popped into his head right away when he thought of a good toad-catching place.

Mike leaned Claire's bicycle against the fence and looked in at the cows. He had always supposed they were nice friendly cows, but then he'd always been on this side of the fence. If he climbed in on their side maybe they wouldn't be so friendly.

He slid through the barbed-wire fence, scratching himself in only two places, and walked over to the pond. The cows stood halfway up the slope of the field, watching him and chewing slowly. One of them lifted her head and mooed loudly and Mike slowed down and looked at her. But then she just went on chewing and watching and he decided they didn't really mind him being here. He went closer to the pond, and all of a sudden the air was full of little whizzing dark things that sailed off the bank and landed in the water, *plip plop plup*.

Toads! Thousands of toads! He could easily find one the right size and take it home. He ran to the pond's edge and more of the things splashed into the water. He could see the little muddy trails they made as they buried themselves in the debris at the bottom. He could even see once in a while a pair of skinny kicking legs.

He made a grab for one that was flying through the air and missed it by quite a lot and nearly fell in besides. Then he tried for one that was in the water, kicking its way through the dead leaves and mud right at the water's edge. But all he got was a handful of rotted leaves and some pebbles. He made his way cautiously along the bank, and in front of him the toads spouted into the water in long arching leaps and grasshoppers sailed away into the weeds in the same way.

He'd never be able to catch one by creeping up on it. Somehow they could tell he was coming before he even set foot on the ground. Maybe they could feel vibrations. Or maybe they were just smart. He found a shady place and sat down and thought. He wondered if he could catch one with a net or a fishing line or something.

Well, he didn't have a net or a fishing line or something, all he had was his two hands. Maybe if he sat there for a long time very still the toads would think he had gone to sleep or taken root like a bush. Maybe they would forget about him being there and come out on the bank, close enough for him to grab.

He sat and sat. The cows chewed and the grasshoppers ticked and buzzed in the long grass. Great numbers of bugs moved around on top of the pond: long-legged spiderlike creatures who skated swiftly over the surface and small brown beetle-shaped oval things who whirled about like mad. On the bottom tiny beasts went feathering through the water and sliding over the mud. Mike watched them, not sure what kind of thing they were. Those on top of the water were certainly bugs, but he didn't know about underneath. Could bugs live under water? Did bugs drown? Yes, they did. He often saw them drowned in swimming pools.

Something scurried away over the floor; a whirling cloud of muddied water marked the way it went. It burrowed down under the leaves and then suddenly shot up to the surface and seemed to snatch at the air and then returned to the bottom. What in the world? Mike was amazed at all the things that were going on in the little pond. He had had no idea.

Were there any fish? A foot or so from the bank were two big things he was almost sure were tadpoles, fat and goldy-brown. But he didn't believe there were any fish.

He tried to sit still as a bush but it was awfully hard. His nose itched and his shoulders itched and the grass tickled his legs. He scratched these places as inconspicuously as he could. The sun moved and struck right on his head, and he was hot and what's more he was sweating and the sweat kept trickling down into his eyes. He reached for his handkerchief, drawing his hand back slowly an inch at a time, only to find when he got to his pocket that he didn't have a handkerchief. The sweat trickled on down and he got hotter and hotter.

He was just about to give up when he noticed something. A dark blunt nose pointed out from under a layer of silt-covered leaves. It hadn't been there a few minutes ago, he was certain. If he could just lean over and raise his arm without scaring the creature, he'd be able to catch it, he knew he would. He'd have that toad in his hands!

Slowly, slowly, slowly, he leaned over the pond. The black nose stayed. In fact it seemed to poke out a little further. Slowly, slowly, Mike extended his arm over the surface. It seemed as though he were taking hours and hours to do it. He could hardly breathe. He opened his fingers, spreading them so wide he thought he'd sprained them. He brought his hand slowly, slowly down toward the water and aimed as carefully as he knew how.

He was almost scared to try. Whatever would he do if he missed? But he couldn't miss, he just couldn't! His palm almost touched the water. "Help!" he muttered and plunged his hand in and grabbed. The warm water splashed all over him and he had to catch himself with his left arm to keep from falling in on his face, but he didn't care. For in his right hand he held something firm and wiggling. He had his toad!

He pushed himself back up on the muddy bank and tried to wipe the water from his eyes and face. Was it a toad he held? Somehow it didn't seem right. It seemed to have a tail. He held it up and just then a loud and terrible voice said, "Little boy, what you doing in my pond?"

Mike just stood there, gripping the thing he'd caught

and scared half out of his wits. Finally he answered, "I'm not a little boy." It was a dumb thing to say but it was all he could think of. He turned his head and stared at Mrs. Thingummy. He'd always been a little bit afraid of her. She was a big old lady with a prickly chin and a cane, and he'd always stayed as far away from her as he could.

"I guess you ain't," she answered. "You're anyhow big enough not to be messing around my pond. Now scat!" She swished her cane down through the air and Mike's insides felt a little funny.

Then Mrs. Thingummy took a step forward. "What you got in your hand?" she asked furiously.

Mike opened his hand. Some kind of animal lay on his palm, a reddish-brown spotted thing, like a lizard but fatter and smoother and slimy. It was most certainly not a toad.

"I thought it was a toad," he said lamely.

"You put that back," Mrs. Thingummy said. "That's a water dog. Anybody who can't tell a water dog from a toad!" She snorted in disgust.

Mike looked at the little creature in his hand. He wanted to put it back in the water. For one thing, it wasn't a toad and wasn't going to do him a bit of good. For another, it was slimy and a little bit unpleasant to hold as it writhed feebly about. For a third thing, for all he knew it might bite or sting or something.

But he very much wanted to get a good look at it. He hadn't even known there were such things as this. He'd spent a lot of time playing in and around ponds and he'd never before seen anything like this water dog, which looked as if it might have come from Africa or some place like that.

Of course, he'd never before noticed any bugs like the ones here, either. Maybe this was a very special pond, or maybe he just hadn't been looking.

He stopped and lowered his hand into the water. After a second the water dog seemed to realize where it was and it went swimming off and gradually sank down to the bottom and out of sight among the refuse. Mike wiped his hand on the dry grass. But the thing really had been slimy, and wiping didn't do much good. He rubbed it on his jeans. Mrs. Thingummy watched.

"Now don't you come around here bothering my cows no more," she ordered. "Nor them water dogs neither. They ain't hurting you."

"I wasn't bothering anything," cried Mike. "I was trying to catch a toad. I *need* a toad."

"Well, forevermore, there ain't no toads around here," answered Mrs. Thingummy in surprise. "What did you look for one here for?"

"There are too toads," Mike insisted. "I saw 'em jumping in the water."

Mrs. Thingummy looked scandalized. For a minute she seemed speechless. "Toads!" she exclaimed. "Them's not toads. Them's frogs. Don't you know nothing?" She leaned on her cane looking thoughtful and then she said, "You come along with me."

She set off up the hillside along a faint path and Mike followed. As she went she sighed and moaned softly and panted a little. Mike wanted to offer to help her but he didn't know how to go about doing it. Once she made a sort of growling noise and hit out at the weeds with her cane, and then he was sure he wasn't going to try to help her.

They came to the top of the hill and went through a gate. She fastened it behind them and then pointed ahead with her cane. Mike went where she pointed, which was up to the door of her house, and she came after him and pushed him inside. Mike had never been inside before. They were in a kind of living room and bedroom combined, with a stove sitting against one wall and a big bed against another and a sofa and about a million small chairs sitting everywhere else. And there were geraniums, pots and pots of pink geraniums all over everything, even the stove, which wasn't a cooking stove, but the kind to keep you warm.

They went into the next room, which was the kitchen and was full of red geraniums, and then out into a kind of long hall with windows on one side and in the roof, and shelves and shelves of geraniums of all colors.

It was a sort of greenhouse, Mike guessed, though there wasn't as much glass as most greenhouses had. It was warmish and dampish and bright, and the smell of geraniums was spicy and strong. There wasn't any wooden floor, only a rough skinny brick walk set right in the dirt.

As they went along, the geraniums gave way to other plants, with feathery green foliage or heavy shining green leaves. At the very end of the greenhouse there were some small palms and a lot of vines growing over and around a concrete trough. Mike could hear water dripping.

44

The old lady stuck her cane in the middle of his back. "Stop," she said, and Mike thought that was strange, for he couldn't take two more steps without falling into the trough. She bent over and began to move some empty pots under the shelves of plants. She mumbled and muttered to herself and finally she said, "Here! Looky here!"

Mike squatted down to look. A small humped object sat in among the flower pots. "A toad!" he exclaimed.

"You mean you know what one looks like?" Mrs. Thingummy asked. "How come you was trying to catch my frogs down at the pond then?"

"I didn't know there was any difference," Mike confessed.

"Well," said Mrs. Thingummy, "you sure been allowed to grow up ignorant. Now you can get away with being ignorant and not using your head sometimes. But if you mean to have anything to do with living things, with plants and animals, you got to know how to think and how to use your eyes."

She was silent for a minute and seemed to be thinking. Than with her cane she pushed aside some of the vines and ferns at the end of the trough, and there, wedged in among some rocks and smiling gently to himself, was an alligator!

"Wow!" cried Mike, impressed. It was about three feet long. Along its lips he could see the sharp ends of fierce teeth. It was the sort of thing you wouldn't dream of, an alligator just living peacefully in somebody's house.

"You know what that is?" asked Mrs. Thingummy.

"It's an alligator," answered Mike promptly.

Mrs. Thingummy shook her head.

"A crocodile?" asked Mike.

"Naw," answered Mrs. Thingummy. "It don't look nothing like a crocodile. And alligators are mostly black. He's green, sort of. And different all over. He's a caiman. Eleven years old. My nephew—he was a sailor—brung him to me from Brazil."

Mike was awed. The caiman had been here practically all Mike's life and he hadn't known it, hadn't even known there were such things.

"What does it eat?" he asked. The old lady grinned. "Little boys." she said, and then she looked a little bit sorry she'd said it. "Eats fish, mostly. Chicken sometimes. Canned salmon if I can't get nothing else."

"Gosh," said Mike. "Does he eat a lot?"

Mrs. Thingummy shook her head. "He don't need to eat much, not getting a lot of exercise and all. Anyway, more he eats, more he grows, so I keep him on a kind of diet so's he won't grow too much. I feed him good once a week and that's all, 'less he seems awful restless. Then I give him some extra and he calms down."

"Could I come watch him eat?" asked Mike.

"Naw," answered Mrs. Thingummy and Mike could tell there wasn't any use begging. He wondered if Claire was going to grow up like that and have bristles on her chin. "I don't let many folks see him just laying there, much less eating," she went on. "It was a kind of lesson for you, see. Caimans and crocodiles are different as frogs and toads. If you look at them hard they are. Use your eyes."

Mike did his best. He looked hard at the toad squatting at their feet. He still thought it looked a lot like a frog. But anyway it was just the right size. If he took it home and put in the terrarium, nobody would ever know. He reached out a hand. Mrs. Thingummy caught his arm. "What you up to?" she asked crossly.

Mike pulled his arm back. He hadn't meant to grab. He'd just been so pleased to find a toad of the proper size.

"Could I have it, please, Mrs. Thin—please?" He wished he could remember her name.

The old lady shook her head. "How come you always want to catch something?" she asked.

"Oh, please," Mike begged desperately. "Oh, please, let me have him. Let me borrow him for a little while anyway. I'll bring him back, honest. Just as soon as I find another one the right size. I'll take good care of him, I promise."

Mrs. Thingummy looked at him as though he'd had a sunstroke. So then he explained everything. Mrs. Thingummy listened gravely, and finally she nodded. "All right," she agreed. "You can borrow him. But don't you let nothing happen to him. I need my toads. They keep down the bugs. I don't like to use sprays and poisons and things. Kills the birds. Might hurt him"—she nodded at the trough. "So you bring him back here quick as ever you can."

"Oh, gee, thanks, Mrs. Thin—gee, thanks," cried Mike.

The old lady picked up the toad and took him back into the kitchen. She wrapped him in geranium leaves and then in wet paper napkins and put him in a plastic carton and fastened the lid on with a rubber band.

"Can he breathe in there?" Mike asked. David was always telling him about how plastic could smother you.

"He's got air a-plenty to last till you get home," she answered. "But you hurry. Don't stop on the way."

Mike didn't stop on the way. He pedaled like mad and almost ran over a little girl. When he got home he just left the bike lying on the grass, though he knew it would make Claire furious if she saw it, and dashed up to his room.

In the big terrarium the two toads sat, apparently just where they had been sitting when he left them. Carefully he opened the carton and slipped the new toad out of its wrapping and lowered it into the terrarium. It panted gently to itself and the others blinked and seemed not to notice it.

Mike already had some broom straws and cheese and cat food waiting. He figured he'd try the cheese first because that cat food was really fishy and smelly. He smashed the cheese up in his fingers and tried to make it stick on the broom straw. It was hard to do. He finally got a little wad to stay on the end of his straw, but as soon as he poked it down in the terrarium it fell off.

"Rats," he said aloud and reached his hand in to pick up the wad of cheese.

Pandemonium! The smaller toads leaped wildly around, thumping against the glass. The big toad gave a curious burping noise and moved heavily from the spot where it had been crouched all day.

Mike gasped. For there, squashed down into the moss and earth, was the smallest toad! The big one had been sitting on it all day!

THE SMALL TOAD seemed no worse for wear. It reached up a little hand and thoughtfully wiped some mud from its face and then hopped out of the depression in the moss. The others had calmed down and were now perching in the various corners of the terrarium.

Mike glared at the big toad. All that trouble for nothing. "Darn you," he muttered.

"What's the matter?" asked Mother from behind him. She'd brought in a big stack of freshly ironed clothes and was putting them on his bed.

"Nothing," answered Mike quickly. He hoped she wasn't going to come and look.

But, of course, she did. And the first thing she said was, "Four toads! I thought there were only three in this terrarium."

Mike rolled his eyes up to the ceiling in despair. He couldn't ever get away with anything.

"I borrowed the fourth one," he said finally.

"Borrowed it!" cried Mother. "Whatever for? And who from?"

Mike thought he wouldn't answer that first question.

"From Mrs. Thingummy with the geraniums," he said.

"Mrs. Dunwoody? I didn't know she had a terrarium," said Mother.

Dunwoody! Now why couldn't he have thought of that? "She doesn't," he replied. "She just has geraniums. Well, she has a lot of things really, but mostly she has geraniums. And there are some toads in with the geraniums to eat the bugs, so she won't have to use poison."

Mother gave him a suspicious look. "I didn't know you and Mrs. Dunwoody were such good friends," she commented. She looked down among the ferns. "Have they had anything to eat?"

"I've been trying to feed them," explained Mike. "But the cheese keeps falling off the straw." He reached in and picked up the ball of cheese, moving slowly so as not to stir up the toads again. He squeezed the cheese around the end of the broom straw again and wiggled it around in front of the middle-sized toad. The toad drew back its head a little and then the cheese fell off again.

"Well," said Mother, "I can't blame them. They're supposed to eat bugs and that doesn't bear the slightest resemblance to a bug."

Mike pressed a wad of smelly cat food on the straw and waved it around in front of the big toad, which looked a little insulted and shut its eyes.

"Wait a minute," said Mother and went out of the room. Mike sat there, twiddling the straw in front of the toads. None of them ate. Mrs. Dunwoody's toad, he observed, was different from Bobby's toads. It was lighter in color and not so spotted. He tried to look at it very carefully, as Mrs. Dunwoody had told him to. Perhaps Bobby's toads were really frogs?

He kept telling himself he'd better go move Claire's bike. If she found it lying on the grass, not put in the garage, she'd never let him borrow it again.

When Mother came back, she was carrying three long pieces of cord. Various lengths of thread, each with a tiny knot at the end, were tied to the cord. Mother pressed a little wad of cheese or cat food around each knot. She did it better than Mike. Then she stretched the pieces of cord from end to end of the terrarium and fastened them to the metal rim with tape. The bits of thread with their little wads of food dangled down inside with the toads and the ferns. They swung back and forth like small pendulums, and when Mother plucked at the cords, the cheese and cat food whirled and danced and spun, looking almost alive. They certainly looked more like bugs than the broom straws had looked.

The toads thought so too. The big toad leaned forward and a piece of cheese vanished.

"Gosh," said Mike, "did you see that?"

"Well, almost," said Mother. "It was too quick for me. Do they grab with their tongues? That's what it looked like to me, as far as I could tell what happened."

"Wow!" cried Mike. "Look at that!"

The little wads of food continued to disappear into the toads. Mother went away. Once or twice a toad missed and once or twice the food fell from the knotted threads, but most of the cheese and cat food melted away. Mike replenished the strings. It was fun watching them eat, in fact it was the only good thing that had happened so far.

But he sat there watching too long. Claire didn't say a word, she just walked up behind him and slapped him on the back so hard he fell out of his chair. So he knew she'd found the bike.

Gloomily he wondered what to do about getting Mrs. Dunwoody's little toad back to her. Claire wouldn't let him have her bike again for weeks, if ever. He'd have to walk out to Mrs. Dunwoody's. It would take hours. He'd have to wait and do it tomorrow, it was too late now. It was close to time for supper; he'd heard Daddy drive in a little while ago.

He put the glass top back on the terrarium and coiled up the cords to use another time, and then he went downstairs.

He hoped they weren't having liver for supper. With the kind of luck he'd been having lately, they were probably going to have liver every night for the rest of the summer.

The next morning, almost before he was out of bed, Mrs. Henderson called up and asked him to walk her dog.

"Sure," said Mike. Mrs. Henderson's dog was a silly little white thing, too silly to be allowed out by itself. It wasn't much trouble to walk it around a few blocks on its red leash, even if it didn't have any sense at all and was always trying to run out in the street and bite moving vans and garbage trucks.

Besides, Mrs. Henderson usually said she'd give you fifty cents for walking the dog for an hour, but she nearly always ended up handing you a dollar, or even more. Mike could certainly use a dollar, to put toward the repairs on his bike. When he thought of his bike he remembered Mrs. Dunwoody's toad and how he had to walk to take it back to her.

"Oh, gee, no, I can't," he told Mrs. Henderson. "Not this

morning, I have to do something. But I could this afternoon."

"No, I'm going to my sister's this afternoon, it has to be this morning. Let me speak to Claire."

"And that's the way it's going to be all summer," Mike said later to the big toad. He reached in carefully and picked up Mrs. Dunwoody's toad and put it in its plastic container for the trip back to its home. It was going to take hours to walk there and back.

When he got down to the back yard, Steve and George were there with their bikes. "We're going over to my Uncle Tom's," said George. "He's going to clean his swimming pool. Get Claire's bike and come with us."

Mike hoped they wouldn't notice the toad's carton. He didn't want to have to explain all that. "Can't," he answered. "I got to do something, I—I have to run an errand. Anyway Claire won't lend me her bike anymore."

"Oh," said George. He and Steve stood for a minute looking at Mike, and then Steve said, "Well, so long," and they went off. Mike waited till they were out of sight and then he started for Mrs. Dunwoody's.

He got gloomier and gloomier as he walked. It was fun helping out George's uncle, at least until George's uncle lost his temper, or George did, or they both did.

And tomorrow Steve was leaving to spend three weeks with his grandparents in the country and Mike probably wouldn't have a chance to see him again before he left.

In fact Mike figured he was never going to have a chance to do anything good for the rest of his life.

He was going to take care of these toads and do arithmetic all summer, every day until school started again. He was never going to have any fun or be able to earn enough money to get his bike fixed. He might as well be locked up in a terrarium himself. He might as well stop at Mrs. Dunwoody's pond and drown himself.

He did stop at the pond for a few minutes. As he came near, all those things jumped off the bank again. He wished he could get a good look at one, so he would know what the difference between a frog and a toad was. He walked on to the edge of the pond and stared down into the water. One of the water dogs moved sluggishly over the bottom. A black bird with red-and-yellow shoulder patches flew down almost beside him and snatched something from the water's edge and then flew away. Someday, if he ever had any time again, he would like to come out here and just sit and look at what was going on in this pond.

Mrs. Dunwoody was pleased to get the toad back. At least she seemed pleased. She took the plastic box with a grunt that sounded pleased, and she gave Mike a cooky, a very dry, crumbly store-bought cooky that nearly choked him to death. But he ate it in order not to hurt her feelings. And as he was leaving she shouted after him, "He eats on Friday."

Mike figured she must mean the alligator, or caiman, rather, and that it was a kind of invitation. He was gratified.

He would certainly like to see that creature eat a chicken or a fish, but he guessed he'd never be able to do it. He'd never again have time to walk all the way to Mrs. Dunwoody's and back.

And Bobby Madison had certainly been wrong when

56

he said those toads weren't much trouble. They were a terrible lot of trouble. They took up every minute of his day. It was trouble to feed them and water them. He worried and worried for fear they were too hot in the sun, or whether they weren't getting enough sun, or how to make those ferns stand up enough to give them some shade and shelter from the heat. He spent lots of time just taking the tops off the tanks and then putting them back, and then running upstairs to be sure he'd put them back.

One time he really did forget. He left the top off the terrarium with the tiny toads and by the time he discovered it the little things were gone! He nearly went crazy looking for them. He was scared to death he was going to step on one, and he got down on his hands and knees and went over his floor inch by inch. Ribby was asleep on his bed and he just knew she'd eaten them.

They weren't on the floor. He looked under everything, he even took the books out of his bookcases and they weren't in there. He was sorry he'd left so much junk lying around his room, it was hard looking through it for the toads. But he looked, just the same, picking up comic books and baseballs and dirty jeans and odd socks and a lot of pieces of different games and some nails and a hammer, and looking all over them and under them and every-where.

Mother stopped at his door and looked in. "What are you hunting for?" she asked and he answered, "Oh, just some things," as though it didn't matter whether he found them or not.

Mother said, "Oh," and went on by, and he was so relieved he just lay down flat on the floor and tried to catch his breath while he stared up at the ceiling—and there they were, right there on the ceiling, or at least on the slanty part of the wall over the bookcase that he didn't know whether to call the ceiling or not.

He jumped up and almost yelled. He never thought he'd be so glad to see anything. But then he had to get them off the ceiling. They'd gone higher than his head and he had to get a chair and stand on it. He put his fingers over the first one and waited for it to fall into his hand, but it didn't. He stood there like the Statue of Liberty with his hand up in the air and wondered what to do. The toads were so tiny and soft he was scared to try to pull them off; he'd squash them or their legs would come off or something horrible would happen, he knew it would.

In the end he got a stiff piece of paper and used it to scrape them off into his hand, as gently as he could. They had left the little damp prints of their bodies here and there on his ceiling, just as they had on the glass sides of the terrarium. He hoped Mother didn't notice.

When he had all four of them back in the tank and the cover firmly over them, he went to his desk and took a quarter out of the upper-left-hand drawer and walked to the drugstore four blocks away and bought a Giant Mellowmix Frostee. Even though it meant he was another quarter short in paying for his bike, he did it. He had to do *something*.

The next day when Mother decided Mike had worked enough multiplication problems, she shut the workbooks and said, "Mike, I don't think those toads get the proper things to eat. I'm sure they need fresh food—all that canned cat food can't be the best diet for them. Go out and catch some bugs for them. There's some kind of horrible yellow spiky thing crawling all around on the day lilies. Get some of those and feed them to your toads."

Mike sighed, but he knew he had to do it. He had to take good care of Bobby Madison's toads. Anyway Mother was probably right. Bugs were bound to be better than cheese and Purr-Fect Cat Food—for toads anyway.

He found the spiky things without any trouble. He picked one off the day lily leaves—and it smashed in his fingers, just the way he'd been afraid the little toads would do. A lot of yellow juice spurted out on his fingers and smelled horrible.

"Ucks," said Mike and wiped his hand on the grass. He went back in the house and got a glass jar and managed to shake three of the things into it. He took them upstairs and dumped them into the big terrarium. They looked very bright on the moss and they began to move about right away. The middle-sized toad took a cautious hop forward. Mike had a qualm or two. It didn't seem fair to stick them in there with the toads, they really didn't have much chance.

The toad crept slowly forward. Mike had just made up his mind he would have to get those bugs out, when the toad stretched its neck slowly forward and glop; there went the nearest bug.

"Ow," exclaimed Mike in sympathy.

The toad drew in its head and then suddenly crouched down, looking startled. It hunched its shoulders and

opened its wide mouth and suddenly the yellow insect once again was lying on the moss, somewhat sticky and disheveled but still able to get about. The toad wiped its mouth twice with vigorous swipes.

"Gee," said Mike. "Oh, for Pete's sake!" He remembered the vile smell. These bugs must taste awful too. "Ugh," said Mike, "poor old toad."

He scooped the yellow things out of the terrarium, using an envelope, and dumped them back in the jar and went downstairs.

"Those toads don't like fresh food," he told Mother.

Mother poked at the yellow things while he explained what had happened. When he finished she gave him a sharp look. "Mike, the yard is full of beetles and bugs. Some of them must taste good, even to toads," she said. "Now you remember what we said about being responsible for these animals. I think giving the proper food is part of that responsibility."

Mike took the jar and sighed again. He spent half an hour crawling around the grass and under the shrubbery. Claire came out and helped. Mike didn't ask her to, she just did. And it was all right. If David helped you, he was always reminding you later. He was always saying things like, "All right, Mike, I helped you carry that chair up to your room, so now you help me wash out the garbage cans."

But Claire wasn't like that. Anyway she never wanted anybody to help her do anything. Even if she was doing something that needed at least four pairs of hands, she didn't want any help and got mad if you offered any. Mother said it was because she was the middle child and Mike thought it was just because she was Claire.

They ended up with two June bugs and some striped beetles and a lot of ants. Mike shook them into the terrarium and put the lid on and he and Claire watched.

The ants all trickled down into the moss right away, and were never seen again, at least not by Mike and Claire. Eventually one of the toads ate one of the striped beetles, but they seemed to be scared of the June bugs, which trundled around the terrarium, every now and then whirring their wings over their backs and looking as fierce and shining as small army tanks. Even the big toad seemed to shy away from them.

Mike had planned to go swimming that afternoon. Instead he spent the time looking for striped beetles.

A few mornings later Steve came over. Mike was startled to see him. "What are you doing here?" he asked. Steve looked surprised.

"I said I'd be home in three weeks and it's been three weeks and I'm home," he answered.

"Oh, good grief," moaned Mike. "Three weeks! The summer's practically gone and I've only been swimming two times. I haven't done anything except multiply and divide and look after these old terrariums. I haven't even—"

Steve interrupted. "Well, at least you've been swimming twice," he said. "I didn't get to go at all, not once. That creek near my grandma's house got some sort of pollution in it and Grandma wouldn't let me swim. And the kids that lived next door have moved away, and Grandpa says I'm too big to chase chickens anymore, and I don't think I like the country as well as I used to."

He stared sadly out the window. Mike couldn't think of anything to say. He remembered how Steve used to look forward to spending part of the summer with his grandparents in the country. The world was full of trouble.

Steve quit looking out the window and started looking at the terrariums. He looked at the big one and then he moved over to the smaller tank and looked at it.

After a minute he said in a grave voice, "One of these is dead."

Mike ran to look. One of the tiny toads was indeed stretched out on the moss, its little round white belly shining upward. It looked so small and miserable, and Mike was feeling so awful anyway, for a minute he was afraid he might cry.

And then he thought about Mother and Bobby Madison and what they would say, and he felt worse than ever.

He picked the toad up by one infinitesimal leg and it dangled pathetically from his fingers. "I think I better go see Mr. MacMillan," he said at last.

Mr. MACMILLAN was a little dry dusty man with a little dry dusty voice. When Mike and Steve arrived at his house, he was just going in the front door with a bag of groceries in his arms. Mike said, "Hey, Mr. MacMillan," and the teacher turned around with one shoulder propping open the screen door and looked at them a little nervously.

"Yes?" he said.

Mike never knew what to say when people said "Yes?" at him that way. So now he just stood there feeling foolish and Steve had to speak up and say, "We brought you something we wanted to ask you a question about, Mr. Mac-Millan."

"Oh," said Mr. MacMillan. "Well, wait till I put the groceries away."

He went on inside the house and left Mike and Steve standing on the doorstep. It was certainly a dull place to wait. Mr. MacMillan had a neat little square white house with a neat little square green lawn and neat little concrete walks leading to the front door and around to the side.

There were neat little Christmas-treelike bushes on each side of the front door and some more tidy little shrubs along the front of the house and a tidy small tree at the corner. Mike was glad he didn't live there.

He and Steve waited and waited. Mike got tired of holding the little plastic box with the toad in it. It was a box that thumbtacks had come in and it said on the top TIC TACS and Mike read it over and over. Somehow he didn't feel like saying anything to Steve and Steve didn't seem to feel like saying anything to him.

Finally Steve poked him with his elbow. "He's forgotten we're here," he said in a loud whisper. "Knock on the door." Mike didn't want to, but at last he raised his hand and thumped on the door two or three times.

Something squeaked and slammed in the back of the house and then Mr. MacMillan said, "Just a minute. I have to put these groceries away."

At last he appeared in the neat hallway and stood at the door. "What is it you want?" he asked.

Mike wished he hadn't come. But he held out the plastic box with the toad in it and said, "This is one of Bobby Madison's toads. And it's dead. And I'd like to know what killed it, because I don't think it was my fault, but my mother is going to be mad at me and—" He broke off as Mr. MacMillan opened the door and reached for the box.

He said, "Ah, yes, Bobby Madison," and took the top off and stared in at the toad. Finally he said, "Where did Bobby get this? It isn't a toad at all." Mike was astonished.

"He *said* it was a toad. He said he hatched it from a tadpole," he cried.

Mr. MacMillan smiled. He opened the door a little

wider as though to ask them to come in and then seemed to change his mind. "You two boys go around that way, to the basement door, and I'll come let you in and we'll see about this," he said.

Mike and Steve ran around the corner on the neat little concrete walk and found a white-painted neat door. Once again they waited quite a while and then Mr. MacMillan opened it and let them in.

The basement was terribly clean and tidy, not full of broken chairs and baskets of laundry and dust and spiders and bottles and boxes, the way other people's basements were. Mrs. MacMillan must spend twenty-four hours a day cleaning up, Mike thought. But perhaps she didn't. Probably she and Mr. MacMillan didn't make much mess anyway.

They went though another door into a kind of laboratory. Mike was impressed. It was great. It was painted white and there were shelves all around with bottles and test tubes and a microscope and jars of mysterious-looking things, and there was a sink with a round thin trickle of water running out of a curving metal spout, and there were pots with plants in them, some tall and yellow and straggly and some short and green and scraggly and some round and fat and some just plain dead. Mike could tell it was an experiment, like the ones he saw in ads that came to the house for his father: BEFORE FEEDING NUTRILOME and then TWO WEEKS AFTER FEEDING NUTRILOME.

There were also many, many books.

Mr. MacMillan got out a flat piece of glass and laid the toad on it. Then he opened another drawer and took out a magnifying glass and stared at the sad little corpse through it. Mike remembered how Mrs. Dunwoody had fussed at him for not knowing the difference between a frog and a toad. But he truly hadn't known there was a difference and she hadn't told him anything to help him out—she'd just said there was a difference.

Mike waited. It wasn't his fault, at least. He hadn't done a thing to those toads that would make them turn into something else, he was certain.

At length Mr. MacMillan looked up and said, "This is a young tree frog, not a toad at all."

"What's the difference?" asked Steve.

In his dry-as-dust voice Mr. MacMillan explained. Frogs were slimmer, sleeker, with longer legs. They lived in or near water. Their skins were smooth and moist, not dry and blotched and warty, like toads'. They moved in long light leaps, not short heavy hops.

"Of course, not all those things are always true," went on Mr. MacMillan in his rasping whispery voice. "These creatures, for instance, though they like to be close to water, often live in bushes or trees. That's why they're called tree frogs. Sometimes as they get older their skins get rough and bumpy." He poked at the tree frog and looked a little bewildered himself. "Some people call them tree toads. But they are really far more like frogs than toads."

His voice droned on and Mike found it very soothing to listen to. He almost went to sleep, only hearing a word here and there as Mr. MacMillan talked about "chorus frogs," "vocal sacs," "larval stages," and "spade foots." This last made Steve laugh out loud. Mr. MacMillan looked pained and then he smiled. "Yes, I suppose that does sound strange," he admitted.

He looked once more at the little toad which was probably a frog, and then he said, "I suppose Bobby got these over in Appleton Park—I've heard tree frogs over there every year since I've been living here. My advice is to take the others in that terrarium and turn them loose close to the pond in the park. This one died of a fungus infection, I think, and the only chance the others have is to get them out of the terrarium and into the open. Anyway, Bobby told me that it was toads he was interested in and these are not toads."

Mike thought that was great news. He was ready to rush on home now and take the frogs to the park. But they had to wait for Mr. MacMillan to explain about the fungus infection and how he would cut up the little frog and examine it under his microscope. And he got out a big book on frogs and toads and made Mike take it with him.

Just as they got to the door, Steve asked suddenly, "Do toads give you warts really?"

"Certainly not," said Mr. MacMillan. "However, their skins do secrete a poison; it has been known to kill a dog. So you should wash your hands carefully when you've handled a toad."

When Mike got home he looked at his toads with more respect.

It took Mike and Steve some time to catch the tiny toads—or frogs, rather—and get them into a box to take to the park. Then they had to walk to the park. Even though Steve had his bike he walked with Mike, because he thought it wouldn't be good for the little frogs to ride in the basket, and he couldn't very well ride and not let Mike double with him. And anyway their mothers didn't approve of doubling.

The day was hot and Mike was glad to reach the shade of the trees around the pond in the park. It had once been a large pond filled with water lilies and goldfish, but it had been expensive to keep up and the park people had neglected it, and now the lilies were gone, the water was only half the proper depth. It was full of dead leaves, and only a few fish were left. Most of them were dark, not gold at all. Perhaps they were minnows. Mike peered into the water, wondering if it was full of interesting things the way Mrs. Dunwoody's pond was.

"Come on," urged Steve. "Get going. I'm starving and we've got all that walk back."

Mike nearly fell into the pond. For there, resting lightly almost on the surface of the water, right in front of his nose, was a frog! A long-legged, green, smooth-skinned, handsome wide-mouthed frog!

Mike nudged Steve and pointed. The frog stared at them for a second or two and then with a jerk flipped down into the water and away.

"I guess that really was a frog," said Steve.

Mike said nothing. It wasn't any wonder Mrs. Dunwoody had been surprised he hadn't known the difference. When you looked at them carefully, frogs and toads weren't one bit alike.

Now Mike opened the box and shook the little tree frogs gently out onto a big tree root. Two of them at once leaped joyously away and were soon lost in the grass. But the third stayed on the root, grasping the bark in its small feet. Mike watched. The little frog seemed to be feeling the bark. It slowly raised one front leg and moved it a little ahead. It laid its paw on the wood with a soft experimental touch,

as though it imagined the tree was going to dissolve beneath it. As though, Mike thought, it had wanted and wanted a tree to climb and now could not believe that this lucky thing had happened and it actually had one. Inch by cautious inch it moved up the trunk, and everything about it looked so glad and happy that it made Mike happy. He didn't even mind being hungry.

But Steve did. "Come on, for Pete's sake!" he kept saying and at last Mike picked up the box and came.

"I sure do wish I could turn those others loose," he told Steve. "I sure am tired of taking care of them. And I don't much think they like it in there."

Steve considered. "Well, I can't believe they mind it much," he said. "I don't even believe they know they're there."

"Well, I know," Mike answered gloomily. "And if I forget it, Mother reminds me. And I wish I could turn them loose."

Daddy took the empty terrarium and cleaned it out and replanted it with moss and vines with shiny leaves and red berries and pretty ferns growing on a piece of rotten tree branch and a tall thing with arrow-shaped leaves. He put it on the window seat in the dining room and everybody said it was beautiful.

Mike certainly hoped Bobby Madison wasn't going to want that terrarium back.

As he was getting ready for bed that night Mike's eyes fell on the book Mr. MacMillan had given him. He opened it and there was a full-page picture of the biggest toad. AMERICAN TOAD, *Bufo americanus*, it said under the picture. It looked *exactly* like the biggest toad, and Mike couldn't help being impressed. It was somehow like seeing a picture of George or Steve in a book, as though a friend of his had become famous. He sat on the edge of his bed and read about toads.

Mike was surprised to discover that females were bigger than males. He went over and looked in the terrarium. So the biggest toad was the mama, not the papa, as he'd been supposing. The toad, as though his stare made it uneasy, shuffled from side to side a little and closed its eyes.

Mike went back to the book. Toads and frogs had their tongues fastened in the front part of the mouth, instead of at the back, the way Mike had his. He poked with his finger to make sure his really was fastened back there, and it really was, but finding out nearly made him throw up.

"Oh, oogh, blah," he said and then went on reading.

Their tongues were sort of hollow. Down in its chin a frog or toad had a little syringelike thing; its muscles squeezed the syringe and some liquid shot up into the tongue and made it fly out of the toad's mouth and smack into the bug that the toad was hoping to catch and eat. The tongue was sticky and the bug was caught the way a fly was caught by flypaper. When the toad swallowed the bug it shut its eyes, and the eyes lowered into its throat to help push the bug down into its stomach. For Pete's sake!

Mike stared at the terrarium and the dark lumps in it that were Bobby Madison's toads. He never would have imagined that this was what happened when they ate. He looked forward to feeding them again.

He read in that book for quite a while, first about toads and then about frogs. All these years he'd thought those were just two names for the same thing, like Istanbul and Constantinople. He certainly knew better now.

He read about water dogs too. The book called them newts and salamanders. They were most interesting. If he had his bike he'd ride out to Mrs. Dunwoody's and look at the ones in her pond again.

When he went to sleep he dreamed about Mrs. Dunwoody, only she looked more like a giant toad than like herself. She stuck out a great long tongue and caught a fly with it. And then she said, loudly but in a funny panting-in-and-out voice, "You ought to be ashamed, keeping them poor toads boxed up like that. Let 'em go, or I'll feed you to my caiman."

Mike was scared. She really might do it. He woke up and it was daylight. Daddy was pumping up the thing he sprayed the roses with, and that was what was making the noise Mike had thought was Mrs. Dunwoody speaking.

It must be Saturday, since Daddy was home. In the summer Saturday always came as a sort of surprise to Mike. During school, the first thing he thought of when he woke up was: Only four, or three, or one, or whatever it was, days till Saturday.

He was thinking about this while he was eating his cereal at the kitchen table. Daddy opened the back door and stuck his head in and said, "Mike, why don't you ride down to the hardware store and get the package of spray Mr. Brown has for me?"

"I can't," answered Mike. "My bike's not fixed and Claire's gone over to Marilyn's with hers. Anyway she won't let me ride hers anymore."

Daddy came on into the kitchen and opened the refrigerator door and looked in. "Oh," he said and took out a can of grapefruit juice. "I've been meaning to say something to you about your bike. You haven't done anything to speak of this summer about earning the money for repairing it. Any time I've had something for you to do, like this morning, you haven't been able to."

Mike looked gloomy. It was true. He was going to be an old man before he ever saw his good bike again. "I know that," he answered finally. "I have to take care of these toads. And I have to work on my arithmetic. Mother said arithmetic was the most important thing."

"Has it helped?" asked Daddy, setting his glass in the sink.

"I don't know," Mike told him. He'd worked hard;

Mother had made him. Lately she'd made him do a few problems every day, even Saturday and Sunday. And he really had tried.

But somehow he figured he just never was going to be able to do arithmetic. He'd been trying for years now and he didn't think he was going to get any better, no matter what. "I'm going over to Mrs. Woodall's and she's going to give me a test on Wednesday."

Daddy opened the refrigerator door again and looked in for a long time, the way he always fussed at Mike and David for doing. And then he shut the door without taking anything else out, or even putting the grapefruit juice back in. He frowned at Mike for a minute and then he said, "Well, I hope you're improving. In fact," he went on slowly, "if you are doing well and Mrs. Woodall thinks you're really improving, I'll go on and have the bike fixed for you instead of waiting till you earn half the money. I know it's been hard for us to get together this summer, what with one thing and another."

"Well, thanks," said Mike. He really was grateful. It was nice of Daddy. But it wasn't going to be much use. He wasn't ever going to be able to do arithmetic.

He went outside and lay down in the grass and thought about his problems. A bug crawled over his arm and he brushed it away. Now that was one good thing, something he really had to be thankful for, he didn't have to catch bugs for the toads anymore. Mother had told him he needn't bother with that anymore. Those ants crawled out of the terrarium and went all over the house. One of the striped beetles escaped from the terrarium and zoomed

out into the kitchen and straight into the cake batter. Mother yelled. And after that she said she guessed fresh food wasn't so important for the toads, not every day anyway.

Mike was glad for a lot of reasons. He didn't like doing it, and Claire wouldn't help anymore because of the way the toads ate earthworms, stuffing the wriggling ends into their mouths. She said it was disgusting.

So, in spite of what Mike had told Daddy, the toads weren't such an awful bother any longer. He fed them, using Mother's strings and threads. And he gave them water, in a bowl big enough for them to sit in, for toads don't drink, but must absorb water through their skins. And he tried to see that they got some sunshine, but not too much.

Still he worried about them. They were on his mind. He wished he could turn them loose. He didn't like it when they jumped and hit the glass sides of the terrarium. He knew Steve was wrong; they didn't like being in there, and they blamed him for it.

And he was always scared something would happen to them, and his mother and Bobby Madison would blame him for that too.

Just then he heard the mailman's truck rattling down the street and then the bang of the lid of his own mailbox. He ran around to the front and opened the mailbox and reached in for the mail. He liked to get the mail, even if there was hardly ever anything for him.

There wasn't anything for him now. There was a letter from his grandmother to his mother, there were two large folders saying ORDER SPRING BULBS NOW! for his father— and there was a postcard for David.

It was a handsome picture of people riding horseback along a rocky trail and the sun setting behind mountain peaks in a great display of pink and gold and crimson. Mike admired it. He turned it over idly to see where it was from.

He hadn't meant to read it. It was David's postcard. It wasn't his. He knew it was wrong to read other people's mail. If he got a postcard and David read it, he'd really flip, especially if it was before he'd even had a look at it. But somehow his eyes just slid over the words and he'd read it before he knew it.

"Hi, pal!" the postcard said. "I am having fun riding horses up here in the mountains. So long. Bobby M." There was a space and then the writing started again. "P.S. You can tell Mike to turn those toads loose. I am going to do geology for the Sci Fair."

Mike had already started running toward the house to tell Mother he was going to let those toads loose, when it dawned on him. He couldn't. He couldn't tell Mother, he couldn't let the toads go, he couldn't do anything. Not till David came home and read the postcard, and who knew when that would be?

He slowed down then, but he went on into the house, closing the door softly and sadly behind him. He looked for Mother and she was in Claire's room, putting clean sheets on Claire's beds.

"Here's the mail," said Mike.

"Ummm," said Mother, who was putting a pillow case on a pillow and leaving her hands free by stuffing the pillow up under her chin and holding it with her chin. Mike never could understand how she did that.

"There's a letter from Grandma," Mike went on.

"That's nice," said Mother. "Put it on my desk and I'll read it later."

"There's a postcard," Mike went on. "I think it's for David."

Mother flung a spread over the bed she was making.

"It's a nice picture," said Mike desperately. Mother glanced at it.

"Yes, it is," she said. "Put it on my desk too and I'll forward it to David. No, wait, put it in his room. He'll be home Tuesday. It might as well wait for him."

Tuesday! That wasn't so far off. Mike supposed he could live till Tuesday. And yet it was far off too, since he knew that now right this minute he could let the toads go, that there wasn't any reason to keep them penned up in their glass cage any longer.

He went into David's room and started to put the postcard on his desk. But that desk already had lots of things on it. David might not see it here. He looked around. Everything in David's room had a lot of things on it. Everything but his bottom bunk bed. That was all tidy and neat and covered with a clean green spread. Mike put the card exactly in the middle of the bed. It showed up beautifully. Nobody could miss it there.

Then he frowned. The window was open. A breeze might blow the card away. He looked around and found a narrow metal rod on David's bookcase. It was a little greasy, but it would weight the card. It was slender, yet very heavy. He laid it across the card.

From the door he looked back. Nobody could miss it.

He crossed the hall into his room and stood for a second staring down at the toads. "Maybe I could just let them go now," he thought. Nobody would know they were gone, probably. And when David came home and said to let them go, he could run and pretend to do it then.

"Maybe I ought to let them go," he thought. They might die. Everybody would feel awful if they died on Monday when they were going to be let go on Tuesday. Solomon Grundy, died on Monday. He bet Solomon Grundy looked just like a toad. He grinned a little. He'd just have to wait, that was all. Somebody would be sure to find out, if he let them go now. And he had to admit he didn't have any business reading David's postcard.

The next two days went by so slowly Mike thought

something had happened to the sun and he was the only one who'd noticed it. It was worse than the last two days of school before Christmas vacation. To make matters worse it rained. He couldn't go swimming or play ball or just mess around with Steve and George or even do the work Daddy had asked him to do, which was raking up the hedge clippings and dumping them behind the garage. He would have done it, even in the rain, but Mother said no. She said even if he didn't catch cold he'd be sure to bring in a lot of mud and trash, and she'd just cleaned the rugs.

Monday afternoon he did get to go to a movie with George and Steve. It was all about some men trying to escape from some sort of prison where they were most unjustly confined. They kept almost getting away but every time—except the last—they were dragged back inside. It made Mike think of the toads, and he squirmed around in his seat and wished the movie were over.

Tuesday morning was bright and beautiful. Mike thought he wouldn't feed the toads since they were shortly going to be out on their own anyway and need never eat any more cheese. Instead he went outside and raked up those clippings. He moved some concrete blocks and stacked them around the heap of cuttings and dead leaves and things that Daddy called "compost." He spent a long time watching some really tremendous earthworms that were crawling around under one of the blocks. He washed out the garbage cans. He called Steve on the phone and talked for a long time. And still it was only eleven o'clock.

He ate two peanut butter sandwiches and drank a glass of milk, and a mere five minutes went by.

Mother was making a pie and she looked up and said,

"Now, Mike, don't forget those arithmetic problems."

All of a sudden Mike wished he hadn't eaten those sandwiches. He felt almost sick. For tomorrow was the day Mrs. Woodall was going to test him on arithmetic. If he'd been thinking about that instead of about David coming home the time wouldn't have got stuck that way; it would have galloped by.

He went into the dining room and sat gloomily at the table, where Mother had left paper and pencils and workbook, with the problems he was supposed to do staring up at him.

He did the problems. They weren't so bad and he had to admit they made the time go by faster. It was after twelve by the time he went back in the kitchen to tell Mother he'd finished.

"Well, I'm glad," she said. "I think you're improving, Mike. Here, have some tomato soup. And call Claire."

They ate lunch in silence, for Claire never said anything and Mike was busy waiting for the clock to move a little bit and hoping it wouldn't at the same time, and Mother spent most of lunch talking on the phone.

When she came back, Mike asked, "What time is David getting home?"

"I don't know," Mother answered. "He didn't know whether he'd be on the bus that gets in at eleven or the one that gets in at three."

"Well, I guess it can't be the eleven o'clock bus," Mike pointed out. "It's almost one now."

"Oh," said Mother, "didn't you know? He's not coming till tomorrow. He stayed over to help set up some kind of project for the next session."

Mike groaned inside himself so Mother wouldn't hear, glared at the kitchen clock, and went upstairs to feed the toads.

At nine the next morning Mike arrived at Mrs. Woodall's house. He'd never been there before. Inside it looked a lot like his own house. Somebody had left a pile of records on the floor and the newspaper scattered around on the couch, and he had to sit at the dining-room table to do his problems, just the way he had to at home.

"Now, Mike, we'll start with these," Mrs. Woodall began, opening the workbook and pointing to some division problems. "These are like the ones we were doing in class before Christmas."

Mike looked at the page of problems. He didn't feel scared or nervous, he just felt a little gloomy and bewildered. All that work for nothing.

He picked up his pencil and began to concentrate on the first problem. Suddenly he straightened up in his chair. After a second he looked up at Mrs. Woodall and grinned. Why, they were easy! They were simple baby problems. He could do them in his sleep.

He could hardly believe it. He could work all the problems, even the ones they had been doing at the very end of school. Mrs. Woodall had been right, he'd only needed some extra practice. He could do arithmetic as well as anybody!

His bus seemed to creep all the way home. It got stuck at all the red lights and then it stayed and waited for everybody to cross the street and get right up on the opposite curb before it started ponderously off again. He was sure he could run faster than the bus could carry him. He was out of his mind, he was so anxious to get home and tell Mother and get Daddy to take his bike to the shop. And to find out when David would be turning up.

Mother was pleased. She let Mike call Daddy at work, a thing he was never supposed to do, and tell him the news. Daddy said, "That's great, Mike," and Mike said, "You won't forget about my bike, will you?" and Daddy laughed and said, no, he wouldn't. "And tell Mother I'll meet the three o'clock bus and bring David home," he added, "He wasn't on the eleven o'clock bus."

David looked different when he got out of the car, some-how bigger and littler at the same time. Mother said, "David's grown this summer, but I don't believe he's grown as much as Mike has," and Mike thought that explained it.

But David looked brown and strong and healthy and Mike guessed he didn't. He must be just sort of toad-colored from taking care of those toads all summer.

Mike helped carry some of David's things up to his room. He glanced at the bottom bunk to see if the postcard was still there, but David had already dumped his dirty clothes all over the spread. Mike went to his own room and sat on the edge of his bed and waited for David to come in and tell him it was all right to let those toads go.

He waited and waited and waited and waited. Twice David came running out of his room and Mike jumped up, but David just galloped on down the stairs to ask Mother something and then came thumping back.

It got to be later and later. Mike could smell supper cooking. He couldn't stand it any longer. He got up and went to the door of David's room. David was down on his knees in front of his bookcase, rearranging his books to make room for some new ones that Uncle Ed had sent him while he was at camp.

He said "Hi," and Mike stood there shifting from one foot to another. "Did you have a good time at camp?" Mike asked finally. He'd already said that once, but it was what people always asked and sometimes they asked it three or four times.

"Sure," said David. "Great." He got up and fetched another book from a pile on his desk.

Mike glanced around the room. He didn't see that postcard anywhere. David had moved the dirty clothes and there was nothing on the bed but a tennis racket and three records. Mike hoped the postcard hadn't gone in the laundry basket. It might get washed and then nobody would know about the toads.

He stooped and looked under the bed. "Looking for something?" asked David.

Mike jumped. "I—I thought I saw a mouse in here the other day," he stammered. What a dumb thing to say! Why couldn't he have thought of something better than that?

David looked at him strangely. "Mice don't bother me," he said. "One night a 'possum climbed in bed with one of the boys in my tent."

Mike let that drop. He stood there looking around, not saying anything.

Finally David said irritably, "Don't bug me, Mike. If you don't want anything, flake off."

"I thought maybe you needed some help, putting things away," said Mike hastily. He was thinking hard. In a minute David would throw him out, and he might never find out about Bobby Madison's postcard.

"No, I don't need any help," said David, sitting back on his heels and staring at his books.

Maybe he ought just to come right out and ask, thought Mike. And then he had an idea. "I guess you got a lot of mail at camp," he said.

"Oh, some," answered David.

"Did you get any postcards?" Mike asked cautiously. "Because George is thinking about maybe starting a postcard collection and if he did he might like any postcard you got."

"I got a few," David answered. "But I threw them away when I packed to come home. There weren't any good ones."

"But what about the one you got here?" Mike cried. "The one that was on your bed?"

"There wasn't any postcard on my bed," David said. "What's the matter with you?"

"There was so too," Mike asserted fiercely. "I put it there." He ran to the head of the stairs. "Mother!" he bawled desperately. "Mother! What happened to David's postcard?"

Mother stuck her head out of the dining-room door. "Mike, don't yell so," she said. "And get ready for supper."

"The postcard," wailed Mike. "The one on David's bed."

"Oh, I meant to speak to you about that," said Mother. "Whatever did you want to put that greasy metal thing on David's clean spread for? What a thing to do! I took it off, and I think I put the postcard on my desk. Now wash your hands."

84

Mike ran down the steps. Mother's desk wasn't really a desk at all, it was just a tiny chest of drawers with a hinged top that unfolded to make a writing surface. Right now it was all covered with envelopes and stamps and a long list of names and addresses, but fortunately the whole thing was so small it couldn't hold much confusion. There sticking out at one corner was the postcard.

Mike seized it and sprinted back up the steps. He handed the card triumphantly to David and David said, "Oh, well, thanks." He looked at Mike suspiciously. Mike held his breath. Would David read it now?

And would he tell what it said?

David looked for a minute at the picture and then turned it over and slowly read the message.

"Supper's ready," called Mother.

David got up off the floor. "It's from Bobby Madison," he said, and put it on his desk. Mike almost yelled. David look at him again very hard. "He says he doesn't want those toads, Mike. You can let them go."

MIKE THOUGHT making a cake was kind of fun. You got to slop around with the electric mixer and lick up all the globs that fell on the table. And breaking eggs was fun except if the egg white got on your hands it was ughy.

Claire was helping. Or at least she said she'd grease the pans and pour the batter in return for one of the beaters to lick, and Mike was delighted to have her do it. "How long does it have to cook?" he asked, and Claire said, "Half an hour. And you better go wash your face and hands."

In the bathroom he could see what she meant. He even had chocolate cake batter in his hair. He grinned at himself. He guessed he'd better change his shirt too, before Mother saw him.

In his room he got a shirt from a drawer and pulled it over his head. As his head emerged from the neck opening, the first thing he saw was the goldfish swimming slowly about in their bowl. They sat right where the toads used to sit, and the sun of this October afternoon slanted through the water.

He went over and looked at them. They belonged to his mother, so he didn't have to feed them or anything. She had bought them and put them there because she said she missed the toads. It was strange. Mike had missed them too. He'd missed seeing them staring out at him and hopping around and even missed them thumping into the glass.

He remembered how much he'd wanted to let them go. The day that David came home and read that postcard, Mike could hardly sit through supper even though it was a celebration coming-home supper with lemon pie for dessert. He'd only eaten one slice of pie and then rushed upstairs and put the toads in a box and carried them over to Appleton Park. He would rather have given them to Mrs. Dunwoody, but he was wild to get them out of the terrarium and he had to let them loose right then. He couldn't wait till morning when he could walk to Mrs. Dunwoody's.

In the park near the pond he opened the box and dumped them gently out into the grass. He walked away from them and stopped and looked back. They crouched there in the grass, not moving, a big toad and a middle-sized toad and a small toad. He watched, and at last, one by one, starting cautiously with little shuffles and steps and then gradually beginning to make longer and longer hops, they went their ways, one into the weeds, one behind a bush, and the last, the middle-sized one, jumping toward the pond, each lumbering bound a little longer, a little freer, a little more gleeful.

He had been right. They had wanted to be out of their cage and now they were finding it just as nice to be out of that glass jail as he'd thought they would.

The rest of the summer, after he had let the toads go, had been great. It really had. He still had to do some arithmetic once in a while, he still had to do some work for Daddy. But he had his bike. He did all those things he'd wanted to do earlier in the summer and hadn't been able to, and somehow they seemed more fun now.

He went swimming and he played ball and he rode his bike. He and George and Steve often rode out to Mrs. Dunwoody's and spent a couple of hours looking at the creatures in her pond. They went to see Mrs. Dunwoody and she let them see the caiman and once she even let Mike see it eat, gnashing its teeth over three big fish. It made Mike a little uneasy to hear its teeth clack together like that.

And Mike made some money running errands for Mrs. Dunwoody, who didn't like going to town if she could help it. He brought her things from the ten-cent store or the hardware store and she would give him a dime. It wasn't much, but by the end of summer he had his bike repairs more than half paid for, because of Mrs. Dunwoody and working for Daddy and walking Mrs. Henderson's dog. Especially after Grandmother heard about his troubles and sent him seven dollars.

The weather had done its best for him. Days when he wanted to be outdoors it was hot and sunny, and days he planned to go to the movies or watch a ball game on TV or something, it rained. And he had been standing right in the Bennetts' front yard the day Mrs. Bennett came running out and shouted that her kitchen was on fire. And once when he was in the drugstore a guy had come in and ordered a Giant Mellowmix Frostee and before Mr. Davies had it made the guy had said suddenly, "Oh, I gotta go, there's my bus," and he'd run out of the store, and Mr. Davies had stared after him and put the last swirl of ice cream on the Frostee and handed it to Mike, saying, "Here, somebody's got to eat the thing." And he hadn't charged him a penny.

Now Mike dabbled a finger in the goldfish bowl, making circles of ripples so that the goldfish seemed to crinkle up and straighten out, and thought perhaps things had gone too well. That was probably why it had happened, one more time.

It was this way: Mr. Bennett was the leader for Troop Thirty-seven this year and somehow he always seemed to expect more of them than he ought to. Or something. Anyway, when there was going to be a hobby show and all the Boy Scouts in the area were asked to exhibit, Mr. Bennett just couldn't seem to believe there were only four boys in Troop Thirty-seven who had anything to show. He kept asking, "Doesn't anybody else have a stamp collection?" and sounding depressed. He almost made Mike wish he'd kept the toads. He could have exhibited them. Keeping a terrarium was a hobby.

So when Mr. Bennett said hopefully, "Well, anyway, I'm sure we can make a fine contribution to the refreshment stand. Whose mother makes a really good chocolate cake?" Mike's hand shot up and he said, "My mother does, Mr. Bennett. She'll be glad to make one."

And that was why Mike was spending this perfectly good Saturday afternoon making a chocolate cake, with Claire's help. And it really hadn't been hard. Claire helped him make bushels of chocolate icing and they piled it on. And he guessed that was a good thing because the layers didn't seem to be as thick as they were when Mother made a chocolate cake.

Just after supper he took the cake over to the Bennetts'. It was in a box and he walked carefully, holding it balanced out in front of him. Mr. Bennett met him at the door and took the cake from him. He looked down at it gloomily.

"It looks good," he said in a sad voice. "Only four entries. Mike, you sure you don't have something to exhibit? Don't you think you could find something?"

Mike almost said, yes, he would. He really almost did. But instead he caught himself in time and shook his head. "I don't have anything, Mr. Bennett," he answered. "I don't even have my bubble gum funnies anymore."

On the way home he pondered over this. It was certainly sad for Mr. Bennett, especially after he found out George only had twelve postcards in his collection and two of them were just alike.

It was a warmish cloudy fall evening, getting dark, and the street lights had been on for some time. All of a sudden Mike spied something on the sidewalk ahead of him, a big dark blob. When he came up to it he saw it was a toad!

There was a time when he'd have thought that blob was just a rock and not paid any attention to it. But tonight he had suspected it was a toad right away. Maybe Mrs. Dunwoody would be pleased that he was learning to use his eyes.

It was a big toad. Appleton Park was only a block or so away. Mike wondered if it was his own big toad trying to find its way back to him. He stopped and knelt down beside it. The light caught its gold eye and made it glow. It looked placidly at Mike and swallowed.

"It's time you were in bed," Mike said severely. Toads, he had read in Mr. MacMillan's book, hibernate during the winter, burying themselves in the mud and under rocks where frost can't reach and snugly sleeping away the cold weather.

The toad said nothing. Suddenly Mike had an idea. He still had the big terrarium. Bobby Madison kept saying he was going to come get it but he never had. It was still full of gravel and earth. He could take this toad home and put it in the big terrarium and set a pot of ferns in with it and exhibit it as a hobby, at the show. It would certainly please Mr. Bennett.

He put a hand around the toad and picked it up gently, putting his other hand underneath it to support it. The toad seemed sluggish and did not try to escape. Mike stroked its rough back, thinking how pleased Mr. Bennett would be. And maybe he could make toads his Science Fair project when he was in junior high. That would please Mr. Mac-Millan.

Thinking about Mr. MacMillan made Mike remember the tree frogs and the happy day he had let them go. He remembered suddenly the sad thumps the toads made when they jumped and hit the sides of the glass box they lived in.

He began to walk, carrying the toad as carefully as he had the cake. He retraced the block and a half to Appleton Park and carried the toad through the shadowy bushes to the pond. He set it down in the grass and gave it a little push. "Git," he said softly.

The toad hopped away, and Mike ran happily home.

ABOUT THE AUTHOR

WILSON GAGE is the pen name of Mary Q. Steele, member of a gifted and successful family of writers; her husband, William, her sister, and her mother, Christine Govan, are the authors of many popular books for children and young people. Her first book, *Secret of the Indian Mound*, quickly established her in the children's-book field. All her books are characterized by her long interest in nature and regional history. In 1960 her book *The Secret of Fiery Gorge* was chosen as an Honor Book in the Children's Spring Book Festival of the New York *Herald Tribune*, and more recently, *Big Blue Island* received the 1966 Aurianne Award of the Children's Services Division of the American Library Association.

Wilson Gage was born in Chattanooga, Tennessee, and is a graduate of the University of Chattanooga. She lives with her husband and three children in Signal Mountain, Tennessee.

ABOUT THE ARTIST

GLEN ROUNDS' first collaboration with Wilson Gage, on *A Wild Goose Tale*, sprang from a shared fascination with nature and her small creatures.

Mr. Rounds was born in the South Dakota Bad Lands and grew up on a Montana ranch "well stocked with horses, cattle, gray wolves, badgers, antelope and the like." He attended the Art Institute in Kansas City, Missouri, and the Art Students League in New York, and has written and illustrated many books for children. His most recent are *Rain in the Woods and Other Small Matters*, and *The Snake Tree*, both A.L.A. Notable Books. He now lives in Southern Pines, North Carolina.

DATE